This Starfish Bay book belongs to

....

LITTLE BEAR'S SUNSHINE

By Bingbo

Illustrated by Jiwei Qian and Daqing

STARFISH BAY
CHILDREN'S BOOKS

In a bright, leafy forest there lived a little bear whose house was inside a large tree. The house had a wooden door and a small window.

This small window was the little bear's favorite part of the house.

During the day, he spent lots of time leaning out the window, looking at the forest all around him.

At night, he stared out the window at the twinkling stars
and bright moon.

But the little bear's favorite time of day was when the sun shone in through his window each morning while he was asleep. The sun shone so brightly on his face that it made his nose itch.

A-a-a-choo! The little bear sneezed loudly and then got up out of bed.

"The sunshine coming through the window is different from the sunlight outside because this is my very own sunshine," thought the little bear.

Sometimes, the sunshine shone on the little bear's face when he was eating breakfast at the table. He would shake his head and say, "Oh, the sunshine is too strong! I have to wear my sunglasses," just as if he were on holiday at the beach.

Sometimes the little bear wore a sunhat or held an umbrella.

The sunshine was so strong it could dry out the fruit, vegetables,
and nuts the little bear had collected from the forest.
The sunshine inside the house accompanied him every day.

Throughout the summer, the little bear ate lots of nuts and fruits and vegetables, and when fall came, he got ready to hibernate in his house for the cold winter months.

Each fall, the little bear closed his front door, made up his comfy bed, and lay
down ready for a long sleep.

The little bear soon fell fast asleep.

Snore, snore...

Once he was asleep, he didn't wake until spring.

However, this year, the little bear had forgotten to draw the curtains before going to sleep.

The next morning, sunshine streamed through the window and shone on his face as usual. The little bear tossed and turned in his bed and didn't go into a deep sleep.

Outside, it was getting colder and colder, so cold that it began to snow. The other animals in the forest were so happy that they built a big snowman.

The animals built the snowman right outside the little bear's house.
It faced his window, as if it were looking inside.

The next morning, the sun didn't shine in the little bear's face, because the tall snowman blocked the sunshine.

The bear slept soundly, and his dreams were filled with happy thoughts.

The snowman blocked the sunshine every day, but very slowly,
he began to melt.
In the end, the snowman was not tall any more. He was a melted
puddle on the ground.

One morning, the sunshine shone in through the window again. It shone on
the little bear's face and made his nose itch.

A-a-a-choo! The little bear sneezed loudly and then got up out of bed.

"Ah, this is my own sunshine," the little bear said happily.

The little bear opened his window and looked outside.
The snow had melted away, and it was now spring.
Remembering his long sleep, the little bear was puzzled.
"I wonder why I tossed and turned at the beginning of my
long winter's sleep, but after that I slept so well," he said.
Suddenly, a little bird flew down from the tree and said it
was because a big snowman blocked his window for the
whole winter.

From then on, the little bear missed the snowman even though he had never met him. "I wonder what the snowman looked like?" he said, and he drew pictures of tall and short, fat and thin snowmen.

Award-winning author Bingbo was born into a poor family in 1957 in Hangzhou, one of the most beautiful cities in China. The name Bingbo, which is the author's first name and pen name, has been used on almost all his published children's books; his family name is Zhao. At a young age, he developed an avid interest in reading books, but sadly, during his teenage years in the 1960s and 1970s, there were very few books available in bookshops or libraries in China. This made his passion for reading very difficult to pursue. However, the few times during his teenage years that he found or was given a book, he would handwrite the entire book to ensure that he could always keep a copy. Throughout his secondary school years, he handwrote around 700,000 words!

Bingbo started to write his own stories when he was very young, and his first children's story was published when he was just twenty-two years old. Since then, he has published hundreds of childrens books, and has won over fifty awards for his work. These include, but are not limited to, the Chinese National Award for Outstanding Children's Literature twice, the Soong Ching Ling Children's Literature Award, and the Bing Xin Children's Literature Award. His writing style is lyrical and delicate, while his books are filled with beautiful language, and his fictional worlds continue to be filled with fantasy.

ABOUT THE ILLUSTRATORS

Jiwei Qian is a Senior Art Editor at Family Education magazine in China. He has received the National Book Award, Bing Xin Award for Children's Literature, and the Best Works Award.

Daqing, formerly known as Xiqing Qian, graduated from the Department of Chinese Painting, China Academy of Art, and has long been working in the field of illustration design for magazines and picture books.

www.starfishbaypublishing.com

LITTLE BEAR'S SUNSHINE

Printed and bound in China by Beijing Shangtang Print & Packaging Co., Ltd

11 Tengren Road, Niulanshan Town, Shunyi District, Beijing, China

Other titles by the same author, Bingbo